Rosie & Jim
and the Rainbow

Written by John Cunliffe

Illustrated by Roger & Sally Berry

**Based on the Central Independent Television Series
produced by Ragdoll Productions**

André Deutsch Children's Books

Scholastic Children's Books
Scholastic Publications Ltd
7-9 Pratt Street, London NW1 0AE, UK

Scholastic Inc.
730 Broadway, New York, NY 10003, USA

Scholastic Canada Ltd
123 Newkirk Road, Richmond Hill
Ontario, Canada L4C 3G5

Ashton Scholastic Pty Ltd
PO Box 579, Gosford, New South Wales
Australia

Ashton Scholastic Ltd
Private Bag 1, Penrose, Auckland
New Zealand

First published in the UK by Scholastic Publications Ltd, 1991

ISBN: 0 590 55154 X

Printed in Spain by Mateu Cromo, Madrid

Rosie and Jim are on their boat, the good boat *Ragdoll*. John steers the boat. What will they find today for John to put in his book?

"Look," said Rosie. "Look, Jim, in the sky!"
"Ooooh, it's magic!" said Jim.
There were colours in the sky.

A band of colours going high, up
and over the sky, far away.
"Hmmm," said John. "A rainbow. Lovely."
"It's blue and red," said Rosie.
". . . and yellow, and orange, and
green," said Jim.

"Quack!" said Duck.
"We're off," said Rosie. "Where are we going today?"
"To find the end of the rainbow," said Jim, "and get new colours for our boat."
"Noggin!" said Rosie. "Look at these trees. I think we're going into a dark dark wood . . ."

"Oooh, Rosie," said Jim, "it's spooky. There might be a *monster* in the wood."

"And it's going to gobble us up!" said Rosie. "Boat, and Jim, and John, and all!"

"Oooh, stop it," said Jim.

John steered the boat too close to the trees. The branches went scritch-scratch, clacketty-clang, all along the side of the boat.

"There's a tree biting our boat," said Rosie.

"Trees don't bite," said Jim.

"These do," said Rosie.

"They're all green," said Jim. "Green and dark."

And he made a picture of the trees in his drawing-book.

The boat bumped so much that the cups rattled in the sink.

Rosie and Jim sang a song.

Scritch-scratch,
Bumpety-bump,
The boat tips up,
And the cups go jump.

Splish-splash,
Jiggety-jog,
Is it a boat,
Or is it a frog?

"There's the monster," shouted Rosie. "It's biting our boat, and it
has great goggling eyes, and a big gobbly mouth!"
"Help!" shouted Jim, covering his eyes up.
"It's only a frog," said Rosie. "Look."
And when Jim did look, he saw a little green frog, sitting by the
water.
"I wish I were a frog," said Jim, "then John wouldn't bump me."
"You'd have to sleep in the bath," said Rosie.
"Ooooh, I think I'll still be a Jim, then. I'll paint the frog instead.
But I can't colour my frog and the trees all round him."
"Why not, noggin?" said Rosie.
"I have no green paint," said Jim.

Then John stopped the boat, and tied it up not far from the shops. And, oh, what a mess it was! There were scratches everywhere. Rosie heard him saying he was going to get some paint to mend it.
She gave Jim a nudge.

"Come on, gobbin, he's going to the shop to get some paint," she said. "If we're quick, we can go with him . . ."

". . . and get some green paint," said Jim.

They hurried after John, just in time to see him disappearing into a little hardware shop. There was a notice outside that said PAINT in big letters. Rosie looked through the window, and saw John getting his paint and brushes.

"What colours is he getting, Rosie?" said Jim.

"Blue," said Rosie. "And yellow . . . and red."

"No green?" said Jim.

"No green," said Rosie. "The silly gobbin's forgotten. He needs green for the boat."

"Oh, Rosie . . ." said Jim.

"Stay here," said Rosie. "Keep your head down."

She slipped into the shop when
John wasn't looking, and popped
a pot of green paint amongst his
shopping. Then she slipped out again.
"Done it," said Rosie.
John was so busy looking
round the shop, and talking
to the man, that he never noticed
he had paid for an extra pot
of green paint.
John went
back to the boat with his paint.
Rosie and Jim were there before
him, sitting in their place in
the cabin.

John set to work to paint the patterns on his boat where all the scratches were. He didn't see a little hand come and take the pot of green paint from his bag.
John painted over the blue scratches.
John painted over the red scratches.
John painted over the yellow scratches.
Jim painted his frog-picture a lovely green colour.

John came to the green scratches.

"Oh, dear," he said, "I forgot to get any green paint. Now what?"

John had an idea.

"I'll make some green," he said. "I'll mix some . . . let's see . . . some blue and some yellow. I think that will do it."

He poured some yellow into a jar. Then he poured some blue in. He stirred them up with a piece of wood. And . . . hey presto! *Green!*

He painted the boat with his newly mixed green paint, until it looked as good as new.

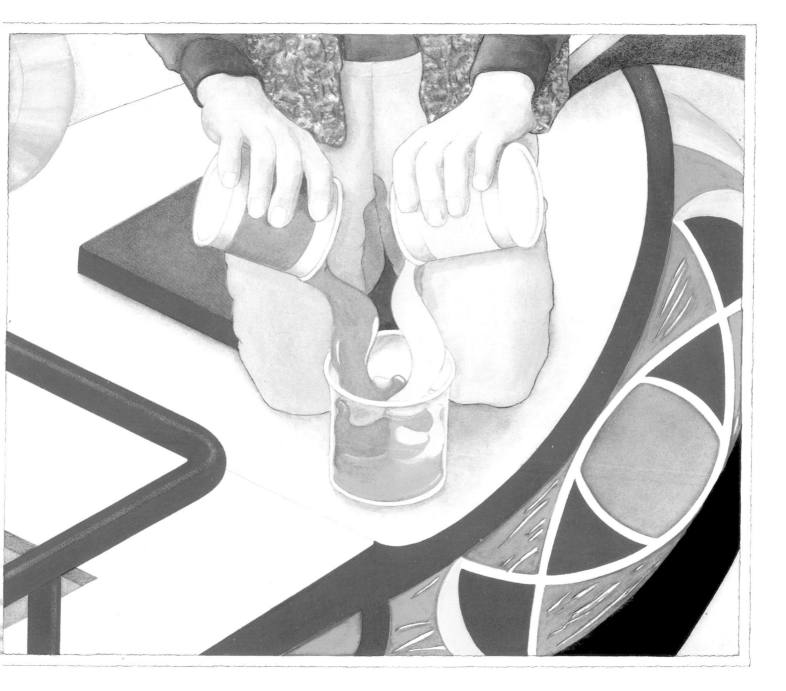

In the cabin, Jim said, "*I* want to mix some green. Now, then, Rosie, how did fizz-pot do it?"
"Ermmmmm . . ." said Rosie. "He mixed two colours together."

"Was it blue and red?" said Jim.
"Oh, noggin, no it wasn't," said Rosie.

"Red and yellow?"
"*Fizz-pot.*"

"I know," said Jim, "*blue and yellow!*"
"Try it," said Rosie.
Jim mixed the yellow and blue, and made a new green paint.
"You've done it," said Rosie.

Jim painted his picture; he painted the trees and the grass with his new green paint.
It was time to clean the brushes and tidy away.

John cleaned his brushes.
Jim cleaned his brushes.
Duck quacked.
"Quick," said Rosie, "he's coming!"
Rosie and Jim sat on their seat, as still as still.
John came into the cabin, and began to write his story. When he
had gone to bed, Jim said, "Let's have a look in John's book."
So they did. And this is the story that they read.

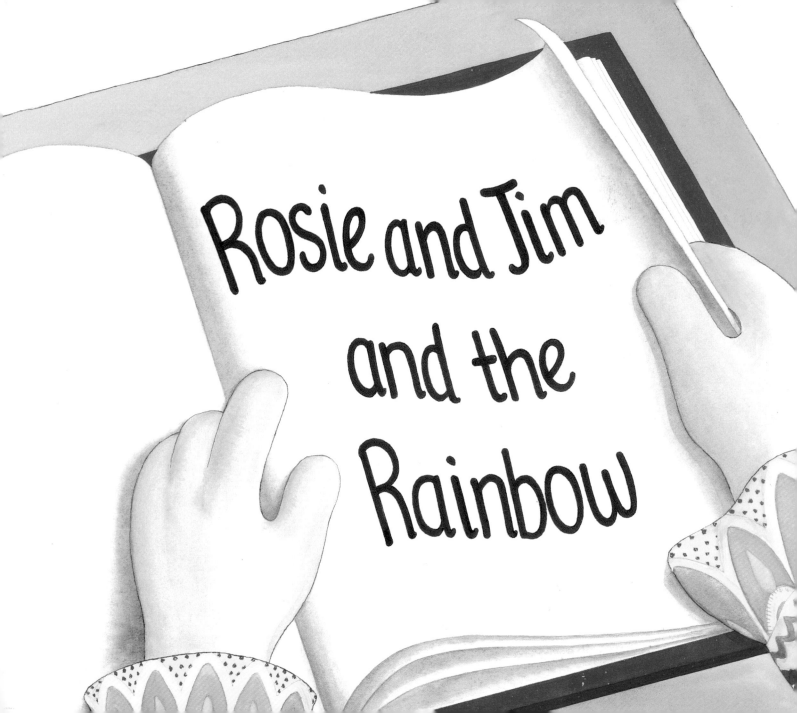

One fine day, Rosie and Jim were chugging along in the good boat *Ragdoll*, when they came to a dark forest. In the middle of the forest sat the Frog King. There were no colours at all. It was all grey and gloomy.

"It's horrid," said Rosie.
"Where have all the colours gone?" said Jim.
"I've swallowed them," said the Frog King.

"*Noggin!*" said Rosie, and she looked up." Look!" she said.
There was a band of colour going right across the sky.
"It's a rainbow," said Jim.

They sailed their boat to the end of the rainbow. There they found three pots of paint: a red pot; a blue pot; and a yellow pot.
"Now we can put the colours back in the world," said Rosie.
"But there are only three colours here," said Jim.
"We can make all the other colours if we mix them," said Rosie.
"You'll see."

And she was right.
Rosie and Jim painted their boat. Then they painted the grass, the trees and the sky.

The Frog King was so cross that he went green all over.
But . . . he never swallowed the colours again.